Christmas '92

GOLDILOCKS

&

THE THREE BEARS

Selected and arranged by Cooper Edens
from the Green Tiger's collection
of old children's books

✦ ✦ ✦

Green Tiger Press

Hardbound ISBN 0-88138-135-7
First Edition
3   5   7   9   10   8   6   4   2
Manufactured in Hong Kong

PREFACE

The Three Bears was first printed in 1837, in a book of Robert Southey's called The Doctor. It was long believed that Southey wrote the story, though Southey himself admitted that it had been told to him by an aunt. In truth, this is an old nursery tale. Southey's version, and other early versions, have an old woman as the heroine. She was changed to a young girl by Joseph Cundall in a version published in 1850. Aunt Friendly's Nursery Book (1850) has her as Golden Hair. She first occurs as Goldilocks in John Hassall's Nursery Stories and Rhymes, circa 1904.

Southey's The Three Bears tells the story much as we know it today, the age of the heroine being the only major difference. However, as she finds each porridge pot disappointing in temperature, "she said a bad word."

There have been many endings to the tale. In Southey's she jumps out of a window when the bears arrive, "and whether she broke her neck in the fall; or ran into the wood and was lost there; or found her way out of the wood and was taken up by the constable and sent to The House of Correction for a vagrant as she was, I cannot tell. But the Three Bears never saw anything more of her." In Eleanor Mure's 1831 manuscript version the bears try to punish her severely, but fail, and finally place her aloft on St. Paul's steeple.

I have approached the illustrations of this book in the same way that I undertook the selection of the images for the two previous books in this series, *Beauty and the Beast* and *Little Red Riding Hood*. I assembled all of the illustrated versions I could discover, and then from each selected the picture which best illustrated each episode. I hope by this method to demonstrate how many different ways a character or scene can be visualized, and at the same time show that many visions can work together as a dramatic whole.

GOLDILOCKS & THE THREE BEARS

ONCE upon a time there lived in a pretty little house in the midst of a great forest three bears. The first was a Big Bear, with a big head, big paws, and a big gruff voice.

The second was a Middling-sized Bear, with a middling-sized head, a middling-sized body, and a voice that was neither very loud nor very soft.

The third was a wee little Baby Bear, with a wee little head, a wee little body, and a teeny-weeny voice between a whine and a squeak.

Now although the home of these three bears was rather rough, they had in it all the things they wanted. There was a big chair for the Big Bear to sit in, a big porridge-bowl from which he could eat his breakfast, and a big bed, very strongly made, on which he could sleep at night. The Middling-sized Bear had a middling-sized porridge-bowl, with a chair and a bed to match. For the Little Bear there was a nice little chair, a neat little bed, and a porridge-bowl that held just enough to satisfy a little bear's appetite.

Near the house of the three bears lived a child whose name was Goldilocks. She was very pretty, with long curls of the brightest gold, that shone and glittered in the sun-shine. She was round and plump, merry and light-hearted, always running and jumping about, and singing the whole day long. When Goldilocks laughed (and she was always laughing when she wasn't singing, and sometimes when she was), her laugh rang out with a clear silvery sound that was very pleasant to hear.

One day she ran off into the woods to gather flowers. When she had gone some way, she began to make wreaths and garlands of wild roses and honeysuckle, and scarcely thought at all of where she was going or of how she was to get back.

At last she came to a part of the forest where there was an open space in which no trees grew. There

was a kind of pathway trampled or stamped across it, as if some one with broad heavy feet was used to walking there.

Following this for a short distance she came, much to her surprise, to a funny little house roughly made of wood.

There was a small keyhole in the door of the house and Goldilocks peeped through to see if any one was at home. She strained her eyes till they ached; but the house seemed quite empty.

The longer she peeped, the more she wanted to know who lived in this funny little house, and what kind of people they were, and, if the truth must be told, a good many other little girls would have been quite as inquisitive.

At last her wish to see the inside of the house became so strong that she could resist no longer: there seemed to be someone pushing her forward, while a voice called in her ear, "Go in, Goldilocks, go in." So, after a little more peeping, she opened the door very softly, and timidly walked right in.

But where were the bears at this time? and why were they not there to welcome their pretty little guest?

Every morning they used to get up early—wise bears
as they were—and when the Middling-sized Bear, who
was also the Mummy Bear, had cooked the porridge she
would say, if it was a fine morning:

"The porridge is too hot to eat just yet. We will go
for a little walk, my dears, the fresh air will give us an
appetite, and when we come back the porridge will be
just right."

And that is why the bears were not at home when Goldi-locks walked into their house.

When she came into the bears' room, Goldilocks was surprised to see a big porridge bowl, a middling-sized porridge-bowl, and a little porridge-bowl all standing on the table.

"Some of the people who live here must eat a good deal more than the others," she thought. "Whoever can want all the porridge that is in the big bowl? It looks very good. I wonder whether it is sweetened with sugar, or if they put salt into it. I'll just try a taste."

So she put the great spoon into the big bowl, and ladled out some of the Big Bear's breakfast.

Now there was so much porridge in the Big Bear's bowl that it kept hot longer than the porridge in the middling-size bowl and in the little bowl. When Goldilocks put the big spoon into her mouth—or rather all of it that she could get in—she drew back with a scream and danced with pain. For the porridge was very, very hot and burned her mouth, and Goldilocks did not like it at all.

"Whatever sort of person can eat such stuff?" she said.

So she tried the middling-sized bowl; and you may be sure she took good care to blow on the spoon before it went into her mouth. But she need not have been so careful, for the porridge was quite cold and sticky. So she stuck the spoon upright in the bowl, and wondered again whoever could eat such stuff.

Then she tried the little porridge-bowl; and the porridge in that was just right, neither too hot nor too cold, and with just the right quantity of sugar.

Having finished the first spoonful, Goldilocks thought she would try a second; and then, being still hungry, she had a third and a fourth and a fifth. By this time she could see the bottom of the bowl, so she thought she might as well look round for a comfortable chair in which to sit and finish all that was left.

First she scrambled up into the Big Bear's chair. It was cold and hard and much too high for her. Next she tried the Middling-sized Bear's chair, but that was just as bad the other way, too soft and bulging.

Then she caught sight of the teeny-tiny chair that be-
longed to the Little Bear. It cracked beneath her weight,
but was just as comfy as ever a chair could be. So she
sat in it and finished up the very last spoonful of porridge.

Then she began to feel very tired and sleepy and gave a great yawn. There was a crack, a groan, and a crash! and down went the bottom of the chair, for you see it was only made for a wee little bear to sit in.

Goldilocks felt a little frightened when she found herself on the floor, but soon got up, and, still being very sleepy, thought she would go upstairs and see if there was a bed to lie on.

Goldilocks climbed the stairs and found, and she expected, that it led to the bedroom. It was a pretty little room, with pink and red roses peeping in at the open window, and in the middle were three beds—a big one, a middling-sized one, and a teeny-weeny one.

"They must be funny people in this house," she thought, "to have all their things of such different sizes!"

She looked at the beds to see which she should rest upon, and tried the big bed first. It would not do at all—the pillow was hard and so big that it kept her head too high. The middling-sized bed was no better—it was so soft that she flopped right down in it. Then Goldilocks tried the little bed and that was just right—sweet and dainty, very white and very soft, with snowy sheets, and a pillow exactly the right height. So Goldilocks laid herself down, with her pretty head on the comfy pillow, and in a very few seconds fell fast asleep.

But before she dropped off to sleep, Goldilocks wondered a little what the people of the house, who owned the porridge-bowls, and the chairs, and the beds, would say if they knew she was there and what she had done.

Soon—very soon—there were sounds in the room below. A big heavy foot went bump—bump—bump; a middling-sized foot went tramp—tramp—tramp; and a tiny little foot went pit-pat—pit-pat—pit-pat. The three bears had come home to breakfast! And directly they came into the room they all three sniffed and sniffed and sniffed.

When the Big Bear came to his porridge-bowl, and found the spoon sticking upright, he knew at once that some one had meddled with it. So he gave an angry roar and growled in his big voice:

"SOMEBODY HAS BEEN AT MY PORRIDGE!"

At this the Middling-sized Bear ran across the room to look at *her* breakfast; and when she found the spoon sticking up in *her* porridge-bowl, she cried out, though not so loudly as the Big Bear had done:

"SOMEBODY HAS BEEN AT MY PORRIDGE!"

Then the Little Bear ran to *his* porridge-bowl; and when he found all his porridge gone, and not even enough left for the spoon to stand upright in, he squeaked in a poor piteous little voice:

"Somebody has been at my porridge, and has eaten it all up!"

He tilted up his little porridge-bowl to show the others, stuffed his little fore-paws into his little eyes, and began to cry.

While the Little Bear cried, th
Big Bear looked round and caugh
sight of his chair, on which Gold
locks had left the cushion all awry
This made him angrie
still, and he growled

"SOMEBODY HAS BEEN SITTING IN MY CHAIR!"

Then the Middling-sized Bear noticed that in the soft cushion of her chair was a hollow where

31

Goldilocks had sat down. So she called out in her middling-sized voice:

"SOMEBODY HAS BEEN SITTING IN MY CHAIR!"

The Little Bear stopped crying for a moment and looked at *his* chair. Then he forgot all about the porridge, and called out in his squeaky little voice:

"Somebody has been sitting in my chair, and has pushed the bottom out of it!"

The three Bears all looked at one another in surprise. Whoever could have dared to do such things—in *their* house too!

"Some mortal has been here," said the Big Bear.

"Yes," said the Middling-sized Bear, sniffing around. "Let's go upstairs."

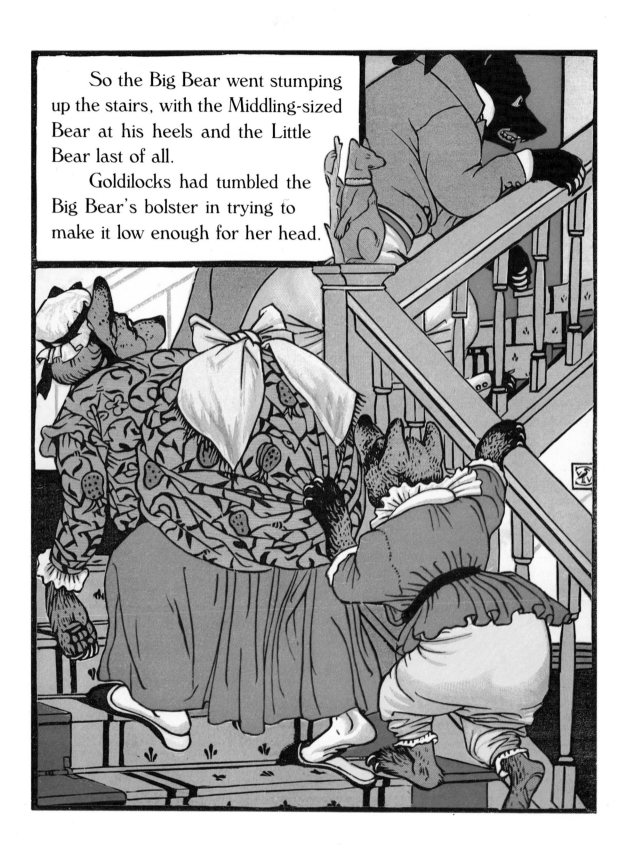

So the Big Bear went stumping up the stairs, with the Middling-sized Bear at his heels and the Little Bear last of all.

Goldilocks had tumbled the Big Bear's bolster in trying to make it low enough for her head.

The Big Bear noticed it at once, and growled:

"SOMEBODY HAS BEEN LYING IN MY BED!"

And the Middling-sized Bear said in her middling-sized voice: "SOMEBODY HAS BEEN LYING IN MY BED!"

Then the Little Bear saw something that made all the hair on his body stand on end.

There was the bed, all smooth and white; the counterpane was in its place and the pillow too; but on them, fast asleep, lay little Goldilocks. To make *quite* sure, he climbed on the end of the bed and looked over the rail. Then:

"Somebody has been lying on my bed!" squealed the Little Bear, *"and she's lying on it still!"*

The Big Bear, the Middling-sized Bear, and the Little Bear all stood with their mouths wide open, staring in surprise at Goldilocks. Then the Big Bear gave a grunt; and the Middling-sized Bear gave a growl; and the Little Bear, who loved his little bed very much because it was so comfy, cried and cried and cried, and thought perhaps he would never be able to sleep on it any more.

Now when the Big Bear spoke, Goldilocks dreamed of a thunderstorm; and when the Middling-sized Bear spoke, she dreamed that the wind was making the roses nod. But when she heard the little, small, wee voice of the Little, Small, Wee Bear, it was so sharp, and so shrill, that it awakened her at once. Up she started; and when she saw the Three Bears on one side of the bed she tumbled herself out at the other, and ran to the window. Now the

window was open, because the Bears, like good, tidy Bears, as they were, always opened their bedchamber window when they got up in the morning. Out Goldilocks jumped into the garden.

Then she ran through the wood as fast as she could,
and never stopped till she reached home.

And you may be sure she never went wandering into the wood again, so the Big Bear and the Middling-sized Bear and the Little Bear ate their porridge in peace all the rest of their days.

ACKNOWLEDGEMENTS

front cover	Florence Choate, *Stokes Wonder Book of Fairy Tales*, 1917
frontispiece	Paul Woodroffe, *Nursery Tales*, nd
title page	Florence Choate, *Stokes Wonder Book of Fairy Tales*, 1917
copyright page	W. Foster, *My Nursery Tale Book*, nd
page 3	Herbert Cole, *Fairy Gold*, 1906
4	John Hassall, *Blackie's Popular Fairy Tales*, 1921
6	L. Leslie Brooke, *The Three Bears*, 1905
7	Charles Robinson, *The Big Book of Fairy Tales*, 1911
8	Eulalie, *Stories Children Love*, 1922
9	Walter Crane, *The Three Bears*, 1873
10	L. Leslie Brooke, *The Three Bears*, 1905
11	W. Foster, *Mother Goose Nursery Tales*, nd
12	L. Leslie Brooke, *The Three Bears*, 1905
13	Anonymous, *The Fairy Book*, nd
14	Elizabeth Colborne, *Stories Children Love*, 1922
15	Anonymous, *The Three Bears*, nd
16	Anonymous, *There Was Once!*, nd
17	L. Leslie Brooke, *The Three Bears*, 1905
18	Anonymous, *The Three Bears*, nd
19	Margaret Evans Price, *The Real Story Book*, 1927
20	W. Foster, *Mother Goose Fairy Tales*, nd
21	Jessie Wilcox Smith, *A Child's Book of Stories*, 1911
22	Walter Crane, *The Three Bears*, 1873
23	Anonymous, *The Milk-White Thorn*, nd
24	Margaret Evans Price, *The Real Story Book*, 1927
25	L. Leslie Brooke, *The Three Bears*, 1905
26	Florence Choate, *Stokes Wonder Book of Fairy Tales*, 1914
27	L. Leslie Brooke, *The Three Bears*, 1905
28	W. Foster, *My Nursery Tale Book*, nd
29	Anonymous, *Mother Goose Nursery Tales*, nd
30/31	Walter Crane, *The Three Bears*, 1873
32	Arthur Rackham, *The Arthur Rackham Fairy Book*, 1913

Acknowledgements continued . . .